Clifford's
Birthday Party

Norman Bridwell

SCHOLASTIC INC.

New York   Toronto   London   Auckland
Sydney   Mexico City   New Delhi   Hong Kong

For Adam, James, and Patrick

Clifford's Birthday Party

Teacher's Pets

This special edition was printed in 2011 for Kohl's Department Stores, Inc.
(for distribution on behalf of Kohl's Cares, LLC, its wholly owned subsidiary) by Scholastic Inc.

Kohl's
0-545-35126-X
123386
04/11

ISBN 978-0-545-35126-3

10 9 8 7 6 5 4 3 2 1   11 12 13 14 15 16/0

Printed in China   127
This edition printing, May 2011

My name is Emily Elizabeth,
and this is my dog, Clifford.
Last week was Clifford's birthday.
We invited his pals to a party.

Mom had ice cream and cookies.
We put up decorations.

When it was time for the party to begin,
nobody was there.
Where could they be?

We went looking for Clifford's pals.

They were all together at the playground.

I asked them why they hadn't come to the party.

Jenny said they wanted to come,
but they didn't have very good presents for Clifford —
not good enough for such a special friend.

I told them not to be silly.

Clifford would like whatever they got for him.

They all ran home to get their gifts...

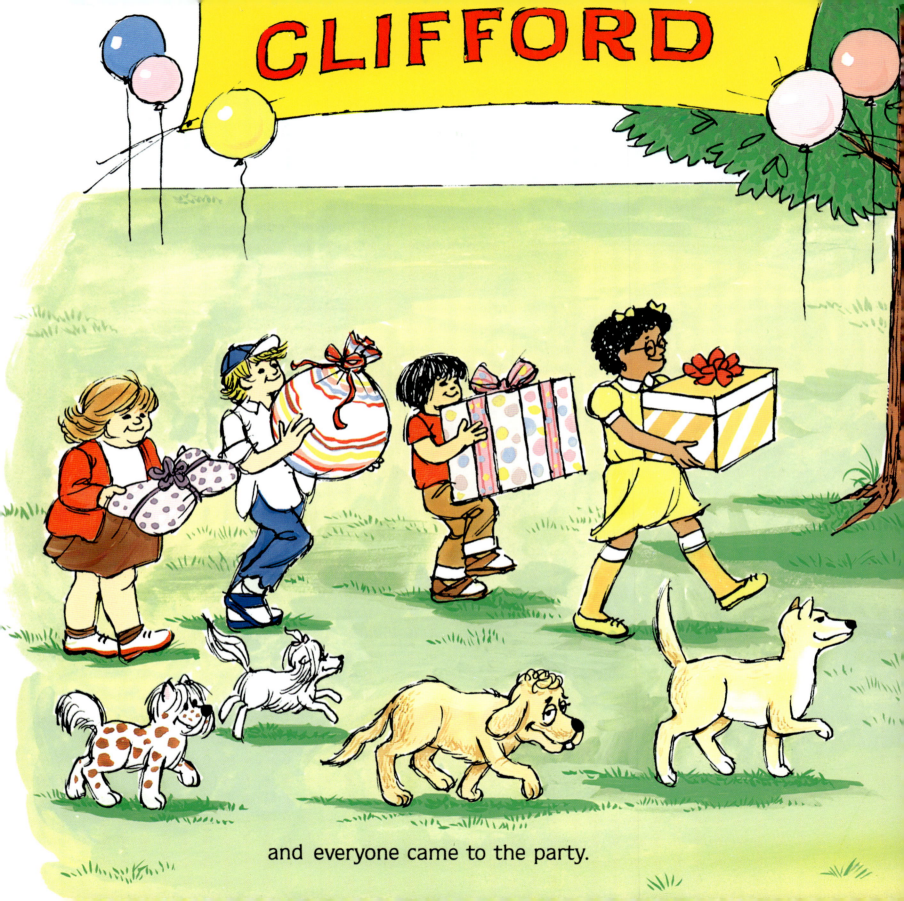

and everyone came to the party.

First we opened the gift from Scott and his dog, Susie.

Scott had blown it up as much as he could.

Clifford blew it up some more.

We really had a ball.

Then Clifford pulled out the stopper.

That was a mistake.

The next gift was from Sam and his dog, Lenny.
It was a piñata!

We hung the piñata from a tree.

There were treats inside for all the dogs.

Clifford was supposed to break the piñata
with a stick.
He gave a couple of good swings...

and the piñata broke open.
The dogs liked the treats...

but we decided not to give Clifford any more piñatas.

We all laughed when we saw the gift from
Jenny and her dog, Flip.
It was a little small for Clifford.

But it was just right for his nose.
Clifford hates having a cold nose.

Alisha and Nero's gift was a toy dog that talked.

Clifford thought it was cute.

He went to pet it.

Uh-oh.
They don't make toys the way they used to.

It was time for ice cream when Cynthia
and her dog, Basker, arrived.

They brought Clifford a gift certificate
from the Bow Wow Beauty Parlor.
He could get a free shampoo and haircut.

We each had our own idea of how Clifford might look after the beauty parlor.

I like Clifford just the way he is.
I thanked Cynthia for the gift,
but I slipped the certificate to Scott
and Susie. I knew she would like it.

Then came the cake. Clifford was surprised.

He was even more surprised...

when his family popped out!

He hadn't seen his mother and father
and sisters and brother for a long time.

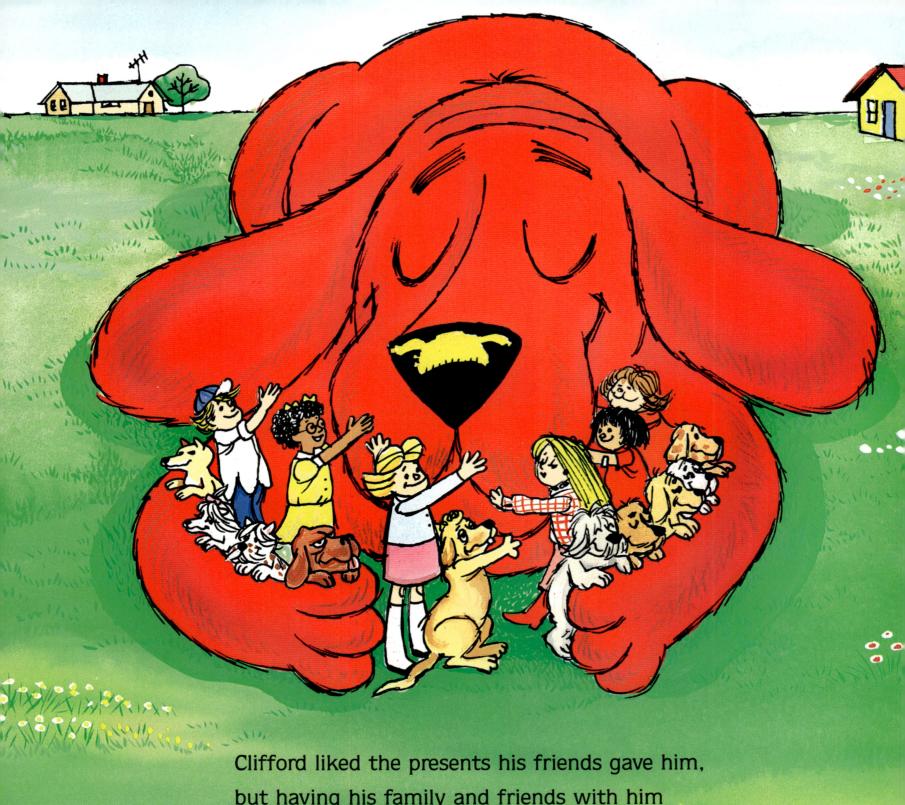

Clifford liked the presents his friends gave him,
but having his family and friends with him
was the best birthday present of all.

Clifford
Teacher's Pets

Norman Bridwell

SCHOLASTIC INC.

New York   Toronto   London   Auckland
Sydney   Mexico City   New Delhi   Hong Kong

"Welcome to doggy school, everyone," said Brittany Spaniel. "We're going to have lots of fun together!

"First, I want each of you to roll over.
Cleo, you go first."

Cleo rolled.

And rolled.

And rolled!

"That's enough rolling, Cleo!" said Brittany, laughing. "Well done!"

"Now it's your turn, Clifford."
When Clifford rolled, the ground
shook. Everyone went down with him.

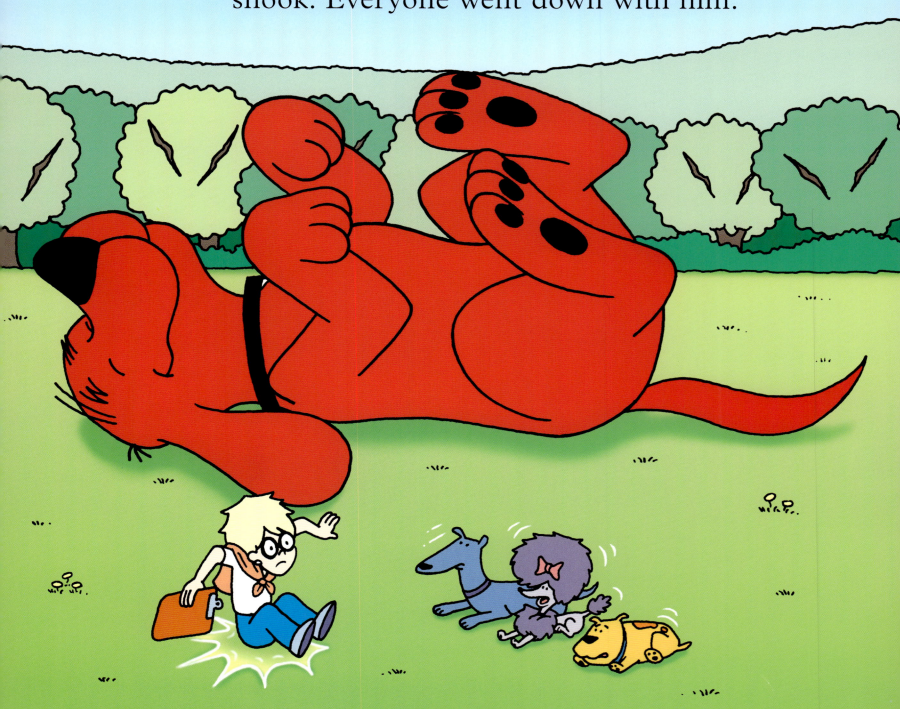

"Wow, Clifford. You make a *big* impression!" said Brittany, standing up.

"Mac, you're next," said Brittany.

But Mac wouldn't budge. No matter what Brittany did, he refused to roll.

"Would you do it for a treat?" she asked.

In one motion, Mac did a roll, sat up, and gobbled his treat.

Brittany laughed. "That was very good, Mac.

"Ready, T-Bone?"

At first, T-Bone was too nervous. Then he crouched down,

did one careful roll,

and smiled.

"That was just fine, T-Bone," said
Brittany as she turned to the other dogs.
T-Bone's smile went away.

Just fine? he thought. *But I did a good
roll. Why didn't she like it? Maybe
tomorrow will be better.*

The next day, Brittany taught a new trick. "Now, I want everyone to fetch this ball. Clifford, you go first."

Brittany threw the ball as far as she could.

Clifford ran and ran, over the trees and into the ocean.

When he returned with the ball, Brittany smiled. "That was excellent, Clifford."

"Cleo, you're next," said Brittany.

Cleo brought back the ball.

And then a newspaper.

And then a stick!

"Cleo, you're doing very well!" said
Brittany encouragingly.

"Your turn, Mac."

Once again, Mac didn't move.

"Okay, Mac, how about another treat?"
asked Brittany, smiling.

Away Mac ran, after the ball. He dropped it at Brittany's feet and gobbled up the treat.

When T-Bone's turn came, he
quickly brought the ball back to
Brittany, panting hopefully.

"Thank you, T-Bone. That was just
fine," said Brittany.

Later T-Bone said, "Clifford, I'm trying my hardest, but she only says I'm doing just fine."

"Believe in yourself, T-Bone," said Clifford. "We all think you're doing great!"

The other dogs barked in agreement.

At the end of the week, Brittany said, "You've all done wonderfully. I'll see you at graduation tomorrow."

T-Bone gulped. *Graduation?*

"I want the biggest trophy ever!" said Cleo.

"I want Emily Elizabeth to come see me,"
said Clifford.

"I want lots and lots of treats!" said Mac.

"I just want to graduate," said T-Bone quietly.

"All my dogs did very well this week," said Brittany. "The award for the most enthusiastic student goes to Cleo!

"The award for making the biggest impression goes to Clifford!

"The award for the best tricks for treats goes to Mac!

And the award for the hardest-working student who always tried his best goes to… T-Bone!"

And that made T-Bone feel just fine!